In The ...

The Magical Beginning

by Paula Lynn Walker

Illustrations by E. J. Bedore

CD Track Listing | Guide Page Numbers

TEACHER'S GUIDE

• A Note To Teachers:

As a young music student, I remember the frustration of learning to read musical notation. It all seemed so black and white and dry. Because of this, I shied away from it, and began to simply memorize each bar or note as I crawled my way through the piece I was learning.

As my love for music grew, I realized that for my creative side to blossom, I needed to know more about basic theory. Thus, through high school, I became more serious, learned the theory and went on to College, and then to University. There, I was able to combine my music theory and history with my passion for music and my desire to nurture the eager minds of children. From this desire came **In The Land Of Staff**, which allows musical notation to come to life, making the Notes' existence important in the eyes and mind of a child… the child which exists in all of us.

The first encounter with any subject is memorable to a child. It is important that the encounter is enjoyable so that the learning process may continue in a positive way.

The Magical Beginning introduces the student to the Land Of Staff, different types of Notes, Mrs. Treble Clef, Mr. Bass Clef, the Music Fairy, and finally, the Staff. Happiness comes to the island as all the different characters organize themselves, cooperate, and work together to fill the Music Castle with beautiful sounds.

The illustrations give faces to all the characters, making it easier for children to get to know them and to recognize their shapes.

LEVEL: This is suitable for the primary grades.

AUDIO/VISUAL CONCEPT: The CD and book should be presented together. An opaque projector can be used. The CD includes full narration, and original background music and songs. Each individual listening excerpt is suitable for class discussion and related activities. I have included the following headings for each excerpt:

• STORYLINE • MUSIC • ILLUSTRATION • OBJECTIVES
• FOR DISCUSSION • ACTIVITIES • VOCABULARY

(These are only suggestions. Choose ideas which are useful for your students.)

Try to set the mood for the story. If possible, have the children on the floor, picturing themselves taking a journey back in time. They will learn about music as well as some moral issues of life.

I hope you will enjoy this voyage back in time to Story Brook Island, where the music first began.

Paula Lynn Walker

2

COME FLOAT WITH ME
Introductory Song

Here it all began so many years ago
on Story Brook Island,
where wishes whispered in the wind,
and dreams were met by the fairies
and returned at a twinkling of an eye.
It was an island where nothing,
absolutely nothing, was impossible.

Imagine the dream fairies
delightfully granting wishes
to all who ever dreamed.

Imagine distant stars
dancing in the delicate skies
and awaiting the soft-spoken voices
of those who wished below.

Imagine, imagine all that is possible
in your heart . . .

1

COME FLOAT WITH ME
Introductory Song

STORYLINE:

"Imagine" is the key word in this section. The listener is taken on the warm, soft breeze, to an island of dreams and fairies, where nothing is impossible.

MUSIC:

With the use of soft **cymbal** sounds and shimmering effects, the music enables listeners to imagine themselves floating. The stringed instruments and other sounds convey a free-spirited feeling of soaring through the air. The music swells and subsides, with the use of **crescendo** and **diminuendo**, leaving listeners feeling as if they were floating on the gentle breeze.

ILLUSTRATION:

The illustration shows the island and the breeze on which the children can imagine themselves floating. The stars are dancing in the delicate skies.

OBJECTIVES:

- To reach the true, imaginative side of the listeners and to allow the music to carry them into the story.
- To show listeners that music and lyrics can inspire moods and feelings in each of us.

FOR DISCUSSION:

1. What is "imagination?"

2. Did you use your imagination as you listened to the song?
   Describe what you saw in your mind.

3. How did the music make you feel? Why?
   Name some of the words you heard that made you feel this way.

4. What do you see in the picture that the words describe?

ACTIVITIES:

1. While the song is playing, have the children stand up and act out how the music makes them feel. Choose individuals to demonstrate. Have observers guess what is being acted out.

2. Give the children key words from the song to demonstrate. Have them do this individually or in small groups.

VOCABULARY

Cymbal
A single brass plate, struck with a drumstick, a cloth-covered stick or another cymbal.

Crescendo
To increase gradually in loudness or intensity.

Diminuendo
To decrease gradually in loudness or intensity; also referred to as *decrescendo.*

COME FLOAT WITH ME
(Introductory Song)

Come float with me on the warm soft breeze.
Return with me to a time long ago.
Let's drift across the sapphire sea
to reach an island waiting for you and me.

Chorus:
Magical, musical journey takes flight.
In your mind are no limits
to where we will climb.

EXCERPT A (pages 2 to 5)
The Seasons

2

Each season,
though it seemed to come and go,
always brought the island sure delight.

With each spring the skies
surrendered showers for the
blossoming of the flowers,
and the silent sleeping trees
began to bud.

With the summer's sunlit mornings,
the songbirds sang their welcome
and the children danced and played
into the night.

3

And even with the fall
there was no sadness at all,
for it was known
that with the winter
soon would come the snow,
to embrace the beautiful colours
which gently lay below.

4

There was one winter day though,
when even with the falling snow
there was no celebration.

There were no snowmen,
or laughing children to be found,
and the whistling of the wind
was the only sound.

EXCERPT A (pages 2 to 5)
The Seasons

STORYLINE:

The seasons — spring, summer, fall, and winter — are introduced. Each season brings something of great significance to the island. Spring brings rebirth and the budding of nature, as winter's freezing temperatures are replaced with warm sun and spring showers. Summer, with its longer days, warmth, and nature in full bloom, invites all creatures out to play. In autumn, the leaves turn brilliant colours and fall from the trees; as the weather turns colder, much of nature is at rest, awaiting winter's passing once more into spring. The falling winter temperatures bring snow which covers everything with a soft, white blanket.

MUSIC:

The music and narrative paint spring, summer and fall with cheerful sounds. Winter's music, however, sounds sad. Through spring, summer and fall, the music is light and melodious to represent the happy changes of season. The free-spirited harp sound is used to help the children sense these positive changes. A light, bright **flute** sound represents the birds in summer, while a playful **clarinet** sound represents children dancing and playing into the night. The fall music begins to change for the introduction of the sad, dreary winter day. The sound of the whistling wind carries this sombre effect even farther.

ILLUSTRATION:

The four illustrations depict the most symbolic changes which take place in each season. Perhaps they will trigger a fond memory, making the children more intrigued with the unfolding story.

OBJECTIVES:

- To teach children the significance of each season, and the necessity for change.
- To teach children that the seasonal changes, each strongly connected to what comes before and after, make Nature's life cycle possible.
- To help children recognize the synthesized instrumental sounds used to represent certain feelings or situations.
- To help children learn to recognize the musical changes from a **major** to a **minor key**.

FOR DISCUSSION:

1. Name the seasons in the Land Of Staff.
   In what order do they occur?

2. What do you remember/like about spring?

3. What can anyone tell us about the other seasons?

4. What is your favourite season? Why?

5. Listen to spring's/summer's background music.
   How does it make you feel?
   Does it make you think of anything?

6. A flute is a wind instrument able to make a bright, light and cheerful sound.
   Why do you think a flute sound is used when the birds of summer are introduced?
   Do you hear any other sound? (i.e., birds)

7. A clarinet is a woodwind instrument able to make a very light and playful sound.
   Why do you think a clarinet sound is used when the children are introduced?
   Do you hear any other sound? (i.e., laughter)

8. Music that makes us feel happy or cheerful is often in what we call the **major key**. Music that makes us feel sad or frightened is often in what we call the **minor** key.
   Does spring's music make you feel happy or sad?
   Is it in a major or minor key?
   Does winter's music make you feel happy or sad?
   Is it in a major or a minor key?

9. How did the music change from fall to winter?
   Why do you think that happened?

10. When you watch a scary movie, do you think the music might be in a major or a minor key?

ACTIVITIES:

1. For each of the seasons, have the children choose a significant occurrence, and then have everyone act it out together.

2. For artistic development, have the children draw a picture of their favourite season. Have them hold up their work for classmates to guess which season has been depicted. Have them give reasons for their guesses.

3. Give the children two pieces of paper. Have them draw a happy face on one, and a sad face on the other. Remind them that in music, happy is often portrayed in a major key and sad, in a minor key. Listen to Excerpt A again and have them hold up the picture which represents the emotion they feel as they hear the music from each season. As they respond to each feeling, pause the CD and ask them if what they are hearing is in a major or a minor key.

TRACK 2

VOCABULARY

Clarinet
A single-reed instrument of the woodwind family.

Flute
A non-reed instrument of the woodwind family.

Key
Tonal centre to which all the notes in a composition are related.

Major
Based on the scale of the white notes on the keyboard from C to C.

Minor
Based on the scale of the white notes on the keyboard from A to A; this is the Natural minor, the only minor referred to in this Guide.

EXCERPT B (pages 6 and 7)
The Disappearance Of The King And Queen

All of this sadness stayed near
because here, on the island, was a land —
the Land Of Staff,
where once the music rang.

It is here that the Note Family lived,
but they lived alone, with no one to care for them.
You see, their King and Queen
had disappeared this dreadful winter day
when the Storms of Sadness carried them away.

Not knowing when the King and Queen
would find their way back to the island,
the Notes were in an utter state of confusion.

EXCERPT B (pages 6 and 7)
The Disappearance Of The King And Queen

STORYLINE:

Left alone to fend for themselves in the cold of winter, the Note family is in a state of confusion. With the disappearance of their King and Queen, only sadness remains in the Land Of Staff, where once there was music and much joy.

MUSIC:

The use of a minor key and a slow **tempo** help portray the sadness of the Notes. The descending bass reinforces the dreary cold of winter, the mysterious disappearance and the loneliness. The listener is left thinking, "What will happen next?" A change at the end of the excerpt, from a minor to a major key, gives the listener a sense of hope and anticipation, and sets the mood for the introduction of the Note family.

ILLUSTRATION:

Standing by the fire, in their winter clothing, the Notes are obviously able to survive on their own, but the looks of sadness and concern on their faces show a need for some mature direction.

OBJECTIVES:

- To show children the importance of working together to survive in stressful situations.

FOR DISCUSSION:

1. Why is this a dreadful winter day for the Notes?
2. Looking at the picture, what are they doing to help themselves get through the day?
3. Notice that the Notes are not too close to the fire. Why?
4. How does the music make you feel? Sad? Happy? Frightened? Think of some other words that describe how the music makes you feel.
5. Do you think it is in a major or a minor key?

ACTIVITIES:

1. Have the children act out the scene with the narration.
2. Have them create a similar survival scenario, or you create one. Let them act this out as well. (Props and scenery can be created, brought in, or simply imagined.)

> **VOCABULARY**
>
> **Tempo**
> The speed of a composition, ranging from very slow to very fast.

EXCERPT C (pages 8 and 9)
The Eighth Notes

The Note family was very large,
and consisted of many ages.
Quite frankly, they were a bit frantic at times.

The half-year-old Notes were very hyper,
and always bouncing up and down the hills.

They were called the **Eighth Notes**.

Sometimes an **Eighth Note**
would pair up with another **Eighth Note**,
and be double the trouble.

They would dance from stone to stone in the brook,
splashing other Notes in the process.

EXCERPT C (pages 8 and 9)
The Eighth Notes

STORYLINE:

The Note family is introduced, starting with the half-year-old Notes, known as the *Eighth Notes*.

MUSIC:

The use of a major key, a quick tempo, and the playful flute and clarinet sounds, show the hyper, bouncy personalities of the Eighth Notes. The two **staccato** melodies represent the dancing Notes in the brook. Using the two melodies against each other shows the mischievous nature of the Eighths as they join together and bounce around the island.

ILLUSTRATION:

The illustration shows the children what an Eighth Note looks like, either singly, or in pairs. The single Eighth Note has solid colouring, a straight back (**stem**) and a curved **flag**. When paired with another Eighth Note, the flags are joined together to form a straight **beam**.

OBJECTIVES:

- To introduce the Eighth Notes as part of the Note family.
- To enable children to recognize Eighth Notes by their solid colouring, curved flags, or joined beams.

FOR DISCUSSION:

1. Was the Note family large or small?
2. What were the half-year-old Notes called?
3. How did the Eighth Notes become double the trouble?
4. What did they do to the others after they paired up?

ACTIVITIES:

1. Note the different hats and collars worn by the Notes. Some are in the style of the **Renaissance** period. Have the children design their own hat and collar in class, using available materials such as paper, cardboard, old rags, and paints for colouring. (See pages 20 and 28 of this Guide for hat ideas.) Then have them act out the roles of Eighth Notes, bouncing and dancing on their make-believe stones or hills.

VOCABULARY

Staccato
Played in a short, detached manner, indicated by a dot over or under the note head.

Stem
The stick attached to a note head.

Flag
The curved tail on the stem of notes of smaller time value than a quarter note.

Beam
A horizontal line used to group notes together.

Renaissance
A time period in music history from around 1430 – 1600.

EXCERPT D (pages 10 and 11)
The Quarter Notes

Then there were the one-year-olds,
who seemed to find pleasure
in marching to their songs;
but, they loved to do this late at night
while everyone else was trying to sleep!

At times, four of the Notes
would begin to march together,
and for each step
they would call out a number.

   "One, two, three, four . . .
    One, two, three, four."

These were the **Quarter Notes** in the family.

EXCERPT D (pages 10 and 11)
The Quarter Notes

STORYLINE:

The one-year-old Notes, known as the *Quarter Notes*, are introduced.

MUSIC:

A march, in a medium tempo, allows the Quarter Notes to march and count from one to four, with their steps. The repeated four Note descending bass pattern gives a sense of buoyancy as the Notes march. This cheerful music, in a major key, portrays the playful Quarter Notes as they keep their friends awake long into the night.

ILLUSTRATION:

The illustration shows children what a Quarter Note looks like. It has a solid colour and a straight back (stem). Unlike the Eighth Note, it has no flag. The Quarter Note is shown singly and in a group. Notice that grouped Quarter Notes are not joined.

OBJECTIVES:

- To introduce the Quarter Notes as part of the Note family.
- To enable children to recognize Quarter Notes by their solid colouring and straight backs (stems).
- To allow children to count the Quarter Notes in each **measure** and to introduce the concept of "one-year-old" Notes having one count each.

FOR DISCUSSION:

1. What were the one-year-old Notes called?
2. What did the Quarter Notes like to do?
3. As they marched, what did they say for each step they took?
4. How do the Quarter Notes look different from the Eighth Notes?

ACTIVITIES:

1. Have the children practice marching, counting one through four with their steps, or have them simply tap their knees (*left, right, left, right, one, two, three, four*). Refer to the CD.
2. Place the children in groups of four and choose one group to demonstrate the activity. Have the group stand in a straight line, and number each child from one to four. Marching in place, each child should say his/her number out loud. This will give them them a sense of where counts or **beats** fall in a measure of music.

VOCABULARY

Measure
A group of beats, the first of which normally has an accent. Such groups, in numbers of 2, 3, 4, or 5 or more, recur consistently through a composition and are separated by vertical lines called *bar lines*.

Beat
The constant pulse with which we measure time in music.

EXCERPT E (pages 12 and 13)

The Half Notes

The two-year-olds
were as mischievous
as the other children.

They were referred to
as the **Half Notes**.

Being two years old,
a **Half Note** would sometimes
make anyone who passed by
clap and hold their hands
together for two counts . . .

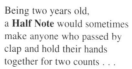

"One, two . . . One, two . . ."

Come on everyone,
let's try it together . . .
    "One, two . . . One, two . . ."

Very well done, indeed!

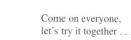

EXCERPT E (pages 12 and 13)
The Half Notes

STORYLINE:

The two-year-old Notes, known as the *Half Notes*, are introduced.

MUSIC:

The excerpt begins with a high **trill**, which gives a sense of anticipation, and a mischievous giggle which shows the fun-loving character of the Notes to be introduced. The time signature is 2/4 (two beats per measure with the Quarter Note getting one beat), and allows the listener to feel the length of the Half Note from measure to measure. (Each Half Note is held for two counts, i.e., one Half Note per measure.)

ILLUSTRATION:

The illustration shows a Half Note directing a child to clap and hold hands together for two counts. The illustration also shows us what a Half Note looks like. It has a straight back (stem) with no tail, and is clear, not shaded like the Quarter and Eighth Notes.

OBJECTIVES:

- To introduce the Half Notes as part of the Note family.
- To enable children to recognize Half Notes by their clear colouring and their straight backs (stems).
- To allow children to count Half Notes within each measure and to introduce the concept of "two-year-old" Notes having two counts each.

FOR DISCUSSION:

1. What were the two-year-old Notes called?
2. What did the Half Notes make the children do?
3. For how many counts did the children hold their hands together?
4. What funny sound effect did you hear at the beginning of this excerpt? (i.e., giggle or laughter)
   Was it high or low **pitched**?

ACTIVITIES: *clap— clap—*

1. Begin counting "*one, two, one, two*" and have the children clap on each "*one*" and hold their hands together on "*two*" and then clap again on the next "*one*" and so on. When they have mastered this, divide them into four groups, begin counting again and have each group clap and count in succession, one measure or one Half Note each.

VOCABULARY

Trill
The rapid alternation of two adjacent notes.

Pitch
A musical tone; the highness or the lowness of a sound.

EXCERPT F (pages 14 and 15)

The Whole Notes

14

Next, came the four-year-olds,
and they were the laziest in the family.

You could usually see one
sitting around soaking in the sun,
or sleeping soundly by the shore,
or even floating freely on the clouds.

They were each named **Whole Note**,
and really did a whole lot of nothing
for anyone.

15

EXCERPT F (pages 14 and 15)
The Whole Notes

STORYLINE:
The four-year-old Notes, known as the *Whole Notes*, are introduced.

MUSIC:
To establish the **andante**, 4/4 time (four beats in each measure and the Quarter Note gets one beat), a **tuba** sound and a bass **saxophone** sound are used. They give a lazy, laid back feeling which represents the true character of the Whole Notes. The sliding clarinet sound reinforces this feeling. The melody is actually a series of Whole Notes played with a high clarinet sound. At the end of the excerpt, the **banjo** sound and the high clarinet sound add humour to the music, as a big yawn concludes this section.

ILLUSTRATION:
The illustration shows a Whole Note floating on a cloud and one lying on a beach, while children frolic and play nearby. It also shows us what a Whole Note looks like. It is round and clear, with no stem.

OBJECTIVES:
- To introduce the Whole Notes as part of the Note family.
- To enable children to recognize Whole Notes by their round, clear bodies with no stems.
- To enable children to see that different instrumental sounds can give us the sense of something humorous, or lazy, or any other sense we wish to portray.
- To allow children to understand that the "four year-old" Notes get four counts each.

FOR DISCUSSION:
1. What were the four-year-old Notes called?
2. What did Whole Notes like to do?
3. Did some of the musical sounds make you laugh? Which ones?
4. How did this music make you feel? (i.e., lazy, tired)
5. Why do you think the music is like that?
6. What sound effect did you hear at the end of the excerpt? (i.e., yawn)
7. Why do you think this sound was used?

ACTIVITIES:
1. Write the names of the different instrument sounds on the board, or if the children do not read, mention the names orally. Discuss what the actual instruments look and sound like. Play the excerpt and have them try to identify the different sounds.
2. Begin counting "*one, two, three, four, one, two, three, four*" and have the children clap on each "*one*" and hold their hands together through "*two, three, four*" and then clap again on the next "*one*."
3. Have the children act out the character of a Whole Note while listening to the clarinet melody. Each time the clarinet plays for four counts, they should change their position (on beat *one*).
   (A demonstration may be necessary.)

VOCABULARY

Andante
Moderately slow tempo.

Banjo
A plucked stringed instrument used in folk and popular music.

Saxophone
Single reed, woodwind instrument with keys and a curved brass body.

Tuba
The largest, lowest brass instrument.

EXCERPT G (pages 16 and 17)

The Notes Cannot Control Their Music

Sometimes the Notes would each
dance and sing their own melody.

Hundreds of melodies
could be heard ringing through the land,
but it didn't sound very beautiful
when everyone was doing it at once!

Thus, a King and Queen
were needed to rule the land
so that the music could be controlled!

EXCERPT G (pages 16 and 17)
The Notes Cannot Control Their Music

STORYLINE:

The Notes each dance and sing their own melodies with no regard for one another. The result is a chaotic, unpleasant sound. The need for a King and Queen to control the music becomes obvious.

MUSIC:

Light, buoyant music shows the singing and dancing of the Notes. It accelerates slightly and quickly changes into confusion, as the Notes dance and sing their own melodies at the same time. The sound adds humour to the story and points out the need for someone to control the music. When the narrator mentions a King and Queen to take over the situation, the music offers new hope for positive change. A **reprise** of the first music of the excerpt, now using a **ritardando**, ends this section.

ILLUSTRATION:

The illustration shows the Notes scattered around the land, singing their own melodies. Although they appear to be enjoying themselves, it is obvious from the young boy holding his hands over his ears that the sound is not a pleasant one.

OBJECTIVES:

- To show children that music needs to be organized and controlled in order to sound as it should. When two or more perform together, someone must be in charge, and everyone must listen to one other.

- To show children that what might sound beautiful to one does not necessarily sound beautiful to another.

FOR DISCUSSION:

1. What would the Notes sometimes do as they danced?
2. Why was the music they sang not very beautiful to hear?
3. The noise of this music made some of us laugh, but how would we feel if we had to listen to it for a longer time?
4. What did the Notes need to help them sound better?
5. What could the Notes have done to help themselves sound better? (i.e., listened to one another and tried to sing things that worked well together)
6. Did the music sound happy or sad at the end of this excerpt? Do you think this meant hope or disaster for the Notes?

ACTIVITIES:

1. Have each student choose a song to sing. Then have everyone sing that song at the same time. They will probably enjoy the dreadful sound which results. Point out to them how disturbing it was for you to hear. Split the class into two groups and repeat the activity with one group singing and one group listening. Ask the listeners to describe how they felt when they listened to the others. Switch the groups and have them repeat the activity one more time.

VOCABULARY

Reprise
Repetition of a melody or theme.

Ritardando
Gradually slowing down.

One day, upon hearing that the Notes were in great need,
a prince rode across the fields and with him brought
great hope and cheer for the children of the island.

Yes, indeed, it was time for everyone to welcome
Mr. and Mrs. Clef, who travelled from afar with
hope of helping the Note Family.

Mr. Clef was a charming looking fellow,
and he preferred to be called **Mr. Bass Clef** —
that was his full name.

Mrs. Clef's full name was **Mrs. Treble Clef**.

When Mr. and Mrs. Clef first arrived, everything was very hectic.
But they knew that things would begin to get better.

The most important thing was to have everyone working together
so that all of the Notes could be a part of making beautiful music.

The Clefs sent for the Music Fairy with hope
that she would be able to guide them.

EXCERPT H (pages 18 and 19)
Mr. And Mrs. Clef Arrive

STORYLINE:

Hearing that the Notes are in great need, a prince, from across the fields, arrives with Mr. Bass Clef and Mrs. Treble Clef. They send for the Music Fairy immediately, hoping that she will be able to help them make beautiful music together.

MUSIC:

A **fanfare**, in 4/4 time, introduces the prince as he rides across the fields to bring Mr. and Mrs. Clef. The strong tuba sound, pumping out the Quarter Note **bass** line, and the **detached**, bright, trumpet melody, give the march a promise of great change and exciting things to come. Strong emphasis is placed on the Quarter Note count (*one, two, three, four, one, two, three, four*). In the second half of the fanfare, stringed instrument sounds are used to strengthen the body of the music, and a light, bright flute sound gives even more anticipation of things to come, as it dances and trills through its bouncy melody.

ILLUSTRATION:

The illustration shows the prince arriving with Mr. and Mrs. Clef. It shows the children what Mr. Bass Clef and Mrs. Treble Clef look like. It also shows the eager looks on the faces of the Notes and the children. They are obviously very interested in these newcomers to their land.

OBJECTIVES:

- To introduce Mr. Bass Clef and Mrs. Treble Clef.
- To enable children to recognize what each Clef looks like and to note the differences.
- To enable children to understand that Clefs are necessary in the organization of music for performance.

FOR DISCUSSION:

1. What were Mr. and Mrs. Clef's full names?
2. Why did they come to the Land Of Staff?
3. What was the most important thing for the Notes to do in order to make beautiful music together?
4. The Clefs sent for someone they thought would be able to help them. Who was it?
5. The music you heard was in a march style. Did it sound happy or sad? Was the key major or minor? *(major)*
6. From earlier in the book, which Notes loved to march? *(Quarter Notes)* What numbers did they call out as they marched?

ACTIVITIES:

1. Have the children clap and count from one to four as they listen to this excerpt. Then have them listen once more and march as they count.

> ## VOCABULARY
>
> **Bass**
> The lower of grave part of the musical system.
>
> **Fanfare**
> A short tune for trumpets, used as a signal for ceremonial, military, or hunting purposes.
>
> **Detached**
> Curtailment of a note at its end either for phrasing or for articulation.

EXCERPT I (pages 20 and 21)

The Music Fairy Arrives

20

Once the Music Fairy arrived,
she agreed to help the Notes create their music,
but only if their purpose be to bring blessedness
and peace to the children of the island.

The Notes promised that this would remain
as their purpose.

She held her special wand and began to create
the most delightful design.

The magic from her wand
left sparkles dancing in the silky skies,
and beneath it brightly shone her creation.

Lines and spaces spread far across
a portion of the land — large enough
that the entire Note family
could join in this joyous wonder;
the wonder that would soon
bring everyone closer together through song.

21

EXCERPT I (pages 20 and 21)
The Music Fairy Arrives

STORYLINE:

The Notes promise the Music Fairy that their purpose for making music will be to bring blessedness and peace to the children of the island. With her special wand, the Music Fairy creates lines and spaces on which the Notes may dance, to create music, and to share in the joys of making music together.

MUSIC:

Sustained string **chords**, one per measure, create a warm sound, and continuous harp **arpeggios** give an energy which foretells something glorious happening as the Fairy waves her magic wand. Shimmering bell sounds heighten this effect.

ILLUSTRATION:

The illustration shows the wand, with its magic sparkles, the wonder and excitement on the children's and Notes' faces, and the Music Fairy's delight as she creates the lines and spaces. The lines and spaces are depicted as flowing and non-restrictive rather than as the stark, black lines and open spaces we are used to seeing. This allows the imagination to run more freely as one moves through the book and CD.

OBJECTIVES:

- To introduce the lines and spaces, later referred to as the "Staff."
- To show that making music together brings the participants closer.

FOR DISCUSSION:

1. What promise did the Notes make to the Music Fairy?
2. Why do you think this would be important?
3. What was the "delightful design" that the Music Fairy created?
4. What was this "joyous wonder" supposed to do for everyone?

ACTIVITIES:

1. Have the children draw or write what they think will happen next. How do they think the Notes will make music on these lines and spaces? Have them draw five lines, with spaces in between, and allow them to decorate them with sparkles. Later on they may place dancing Notes on this drawing.

VOCABULARY

Chord
Three or more pitches sounded simultaneously.

Arpeggio
Notes of a chord played in succession, or broken.

EXCERPT J (pages 22 and 23)
The Notes Create Music On The Lines And Spaces

22

You see, the Notes created the music by
dancing on these lines and in these spaces.

Each time one of the Notes
would dance on a line or in a space,
a musical sound could be heard.
Something like this: " . . . " or this " . . . "
or even this " . . . "

These music sounds were called **Pitches**.

If enough **Pitches** were danced upon,
a beautiful melody could be heard.

Something like this . . .

23

EXCERPT J (pages 22 and 23)
The Notes Create Music On The Lines And Spaces

STORYLINE:

The Notes danced on the lines and spaces, creating musical sounds called *pitches*. If enough of these pitches were produced, a beautiful melody could be heard.

MUSIC:

A bouncy, light melody, in 6/8 time, using **pizzicato** string sounds, gives the listener a sense of the Notes dancing. Single, plucked sounds represent three examples of pitches introduced by the narrator. Following is a short piece used as an example of music that could be created if the Notes danced on enough of the lines and spaces.

ILLUSTRATION:

The illustration shows Notes dancing on the lines and spaces as the children watch. The happiness on all of the faces is evident, as is the passion for learning to make sweet music, and the joys to be found in working together.

OBJECTIVES:

- To show how the Notes created their music.
- To show that each line and space represents a different pitch.
- To show that making music requires some physical effort, but is enjoyable nonetheless.

FOR DISCUSSION:

1. How did the Notes create music on the lines and in the spaces?
2. What were the musical sounds called?
3. If enough pitches were created, what could be heard?
4. Do the Notes have to make a physical effort to create music? Does it look like fun anyway?

ACTIVITIES:

1. Using the lines and spaces drawing from the previous excerpt, have the children place a Note on a line or space and fill in some background scenery as well.

EXCERPT K (pages 24 and 25)
Building The Music Castle

24

In order to protect this creation from the Storms of Sadness, the Notes and the children on the island worked hard together to build an enormous castle.

They called it the Music Castle.

EXCERPT K (pages 24 and 25)
Building The Music Castle

STORYLINE:

To protect the lines and spaces from the Storms of Sadness, the Notes and the children build the Music Castle with the help of the Music Fairy.

MUSIC:

A stately 4/4 march played by strong brass sounds gives the sense of the strength and hard work required to build an enormous castle around the lines and spaces. The uplifting spirit of the march gives the sense of something positive coming out of the toil of everyone working together.

ILLUSTRATION:

The illustration shows everyone working together, cooperating and enjoying themselves as they all strive towards a common goal.

OBJECTIVES:

- To show that there is strength in numbers and power in positive purpose.

FOR DISCUSSION:

1. What did everyone do to protect the lines and spaces from the Storms of Sadness?
2. How were they able to achieve the building of this enormous castle?
3. What did they name the castle?
4. Looking at specific characters in the illustration, what do you think the character is thinking and feeling?
5. Is it important for everyone to try and make the best of hard work? Why?
6. How would you feel if you had to work with someone who was unhappy in what he/she was doing?

   What would you do to help him/her enjoy the work more? (i.e., tell a joke, help the person to finish more quickly, show that you are enjoying yourself)

ACTIVITIES:

1. Have the children list some activities (tasks, chores) they do not enjoy (i.e., washing dishes, laundry, bed-making). What could they do to make the tasks more enjoyable? (i.e., sing, listen to music, think about fun things to do when the task is completed)

2. Have each student choose one of the activities and suggestions for making it more enjoyable, and actually try it out at home. Follow up on this and see how the children react to the activity. Did it make a difference to their attitudes towards the task? Suggest that helping a parent or friend to finish a task sooner may be gratifying to them also.

EXCERPT L (pages 26 and 27)

The Completion Of The Music Castle

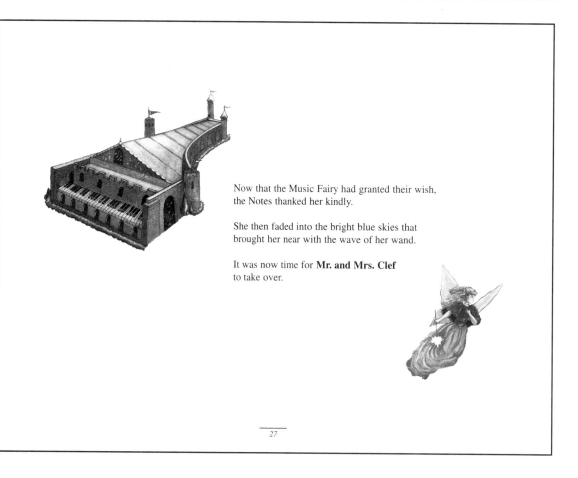

Now that the Music Fairy had granted their wish,
the Notes thanked her kindly.

She then faded into the bright blue skies that
brought her near with the wave of her wand.

It was now time for **Mr. and Mrs. Clef**
to take over.

EXCERPT L (pages 26 and 27)
The Completion Of The Music Castle

STORYLINE:

With the completion of the Music Castle, the Music Fairy takes her leave, and Mr. and Mrs. Clef take over.

MUSIC:

A reprise of the Music Fairy's music from Excerpt I opens this section, reminding us of her purpose for coming, and announcing her departure now that her job is done. A reprise of the march from Excerpt K, thematically reintroduces the Clefs, who will now take over to organize the music on the lines and spaces.

ILLUSTRATION:

As the Music Fairy floats away, attention is focused on the Music Castle, with its unique shape, much like that of an antique grand piano or **harpsichord**. The detail of the castle points out to the reader that much hard work has gone into the construction of the building. It looks very inviting and hopefully makes the reader eager to experience what will happen within its walls.

OBJECTIVES:

• To introduce the reader to the Music Castle and to show what can result from hard work and cooperative effort.

FOR DISCUSSION:

1. Why did The Music Fairy leave?
2. Who was to take over for her?
3. Does the Music Castle look like anything you have seen before? (*piano, but a very early version*)
4. The Music Castle has many windows. Why do you think that might be important? (*for everyone across the island to hear the sounds of the music*)

ACTIVITIES:

1. Have the children draw their own Music Castle.
2. Listen to the excerpt again, focusing on the music. Have the children point out the different sound effects they hear as the Music Fairy leaves (harp sound, the tinkling of the magic wand). Now focus on the march, when the Clefs are reintroduced. Compare the two different moods created.

Music Fairy music	**Mr. And Mrs. Clef music**
light, pretty, magical	march, rhythmic, structured

VOCABULARY:

Harpsichord
A keyboard instrument in which the strings are plucked.

EXCERPT M (pages 28 and 29)

Everyone Gathers In The Castle

28

Mrs. Treble Clef was in charge of directing
the children on the upper section of lines and spaces
and **Mr. Bass Clef** on the bottom.

All would gather in the Music Castle and
await their turn to dance on the **Pitches**.

29

EXCERPT M (pages 28 and 29)
Everyone Gathers In The Castle

STORYLINE:

All of the Notes gathered in the castle waiting their turn to dance upon the pitches. Mrs. Treble Clef directed the Notes on the upper section of the lines and spaces. Mr. Bass Clef directed the Notes on the bottom.

MUSIC:

Broken chords move up the piano keyboard, from **middle C** (higher in pitch), as Mrs. Treble Clef's duties are introduced. (Moving up through the lines and spaces produces higher pitches.) Mr. Bass Clef's duties are represented by the same broken chords moving down the keyboard from middle C (lower in pitch).

ILLUSTRATION:

The illustration shows the lines and spaces as they appear in the Music Castle. The look of joy and anticipation on all of the faces shows how eager everyone is to participate in a musical experience.

OBJECTIVES:

• To teach the importance of the Clefs in music.

FOR DISCUSSION:

1. What section of the lines and spaces was Mrs. Treble Clef in charge of directing? Mr. Bass Clef?

2. As the children watched, what did the Notes wait their turn to do?

3. When the narrator introduces Mrs. Treble Clef, does the music go higher or lower? Mr. Bass Clef?

4. What do you think will happen to the pitches as the Notes dance up through the lines and spaces under Mrs. Treble Clef's direction?

5. What do you think will happen to the pitches as the Notes dance down through the lines and spaces under Mr. Bass Clef's direction?

ACTIVITIES:

1. Draw a Treble and a Bass Clef on the board for the children to see. The Treble Clef can be done two ways, in one continuous line starting from the base of the tail, or in two parts, starting at the top with a "J" and then, lifting, returning to the top to complete the curved section. When doing the Bass Clef, be sure to remember the two dots.

2. Having shown them how to draw the Clefs, have the children try. Stress that it is not necessary to include the faces which appear in the book. They are only to help bring the characters to life for the sake of the story.

3. If a piano is available, play any patterns of keys, up or down, and have the children respond physically by walking and reaching up as pitches ascend, or crouching or crawling as pitches descend.

VOCABULARY:

Middle C
The C which sits between the Treble and Bass Clef of the Staff, and in the middle of the keyboard.

30

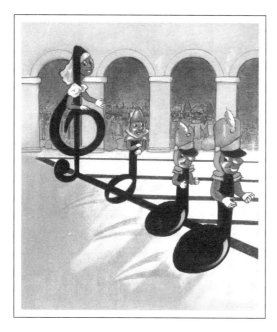

Mrs. Treble Clef would say . . .
"Okay, I would like one of the **Quarter Notes**
in my first space, another one on my second line,
and, let me see now, a **Half Note** in my third space."

Each would get into a line immediately
and go to their positions; but only in the order
that they were told. There were also rules
to making music — the Notes could only stay
on a line or in a space for the length of their age.

So, **Quarter Notes** could stay for one count,
since they were one year old.

Half Notes could stay for two counts,
since they were two years old, and so on.

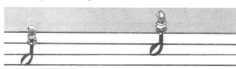

But, one of the luckiest of all was a **Whole Note**,
of course, since a **Whole Note** was four years old.

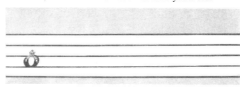

31

EXCERPT N (pages 30 and 31)
Rules For Making Music

STORYLINE:

Mrs. Treble Clef directs some of the Notes to go to specific lines and spaces, and the Notes learn that they may only stay in position for the number of counts corresponding to their ages.

MUSIC:

The music is simple so that the narrator can be heard clearly. It is in 4/4 time, beginning with a piano trill, followed by a single Note melody on the piano. String sounds are added when the narrator begins to explain the rules. Listen for the clicks: one for the Quarter Notes, two for the Half Notes, and four for the Whole Notes.

ILLUSTRATION:

The illustration shows the Notes hurrying into position. Once they are in position, we can see that four Quarter Notes have the same time value as two Half Notes or one Whole Note.

OBJECTIVES:

• To teach the children some simple Note values.

FOR DISCUSSION:

1. What did the Notes do when directed by Mrs. Treble Clef?
   (They lined up immediately.)

2. After lining up, where did they go?
   (They went to their specified line or space, in the order which Mrs. Clef had dictated.)

3. What were the rules for staying in position?

4. How long could a Quarter Note stay? A Half Note?

5. Who were the luckiest Notes of all? Why?

6. What would happen if the Notes didn't follow the rules?
   (The music would get out of control again.)

ACTIVITIES:

1. As you did when the Notes were first introduced, have the children clap and hold their hands together for the correct number of counts for a Quarter, Half, or Whole Note. When they feel comfortable with the different Note values, you could split them into groups representing the different Notes and do some combined clapping activities. Write Notes on the board for them to follow. (In all these activities you must establish a regular count for them to work with — *one, two, three, four, one, two, three, four.*)

2. Instead of clapping, you can have the students pretend to dance on imaginary lines and spaces, stepping and holding for the correct number of counts.

EXCERPT O (pages 32 and 33)

The Music Fairy Returns

32

One warm sunny day,
when the Notes were dancing in the castle,
a bright light appeared in the distance.
While it gently made its way towards them,
angelic voices touched the wind
and whispered their welcome.
The Music Fairy had returned,
bringing a message.
She spoke softly . . .

"I have given you the gift of music,
and you have used it well.
Now it is time for you to find
the music within yourselves."

She then smiled sweetly,
waved her wand,
and disappeared into the soft shadows,
singing her farewell.

Her spell had taken away the sounds
that once rang from the lines and spaces.
The land was silent, and again
sadness filled the hearts of everyone.

They feared they would never find the music again.
The Notes searched within themselves to find
the answer, but still could not understand why
the Music Fairy had taken from them the sounds
that had once soothed their saddened hearts.

Months passed quickly, but they could still
not find a way to fulfill this emptiness.
They would often sit and ponder, to reflect
on what the Fairy had said to them . . .
" . . . now it is time for you to find
the music within yourselves."
"What did she mean?" they wondered.
Until, one day, it came to them . . .
"If we must find the music within ourselves,
then surely, it must come from within our hearts,"
said a **Whole Note**.

And it wasn't long before they realized
what the Fairy was trying to say:
the music could only be found within their hearts,
and could be expressed with their own voices.

The wondrous gift of song had been
hidden within them from the beginning,
and it was time to bring back the sweet songs
that once rang through the land.
(*I Am The Sweet Song*) . . .

33

EXCERPT O (pages 32 and 33)
The Music Fairy Returns

STORYLINE:

The Music Fairy returns with a message: "I have given you the gift of music…it is time for you to find the music within yourselves." Having said this, she removes the sounds from the lines and spaces and disappears. The Notes realize, after much thought, that they can produce music through singing. Immediately, sound is restored within the castle and the Notes and the children celebrate in song *(I Am The Sweet Song)*.

MUSIC:

Full orchestra sounds with rich harmonies, in a major key, and a beautiful singing melody, welcome the Music Fairy's return. This section is in **ostinato** form, with the same harmonic and melodic ideas repeated every 4 measures. As the Notes try to understand what the Music Fairy has told them, the orchestra sounds are replaced by simple harp lines. The orchestra sounds reappear as the Notes solve the puzzle, and the music leads into the song of celebration, performed by the Notes and the children together. (Lyrics are on page 39 of this Guide.)

ILLUSTRATION:

The bewilderment on the Notes' faces as the Music Fairy delivers her message is replaced by relief and happiness on page 33 of the story book, as they realize that they can also make music through singing.

OBJECTIVES:

- To show that the Music Fairy was not taking something away, but rather giving them something new… a realization of their hidden talents or gifts.
- To show that things are always changing, and that understanding why is not always easy, but that by searching with one's heart and mind, the answer found can make things even better.

FOR DISCUSSION:

1. What was the Music Fairy's message?
2. What did the Notes do to try to understand her message?
3. What did they finally realize?
4. Why did the Music Fairy take the sounds from the lines and spaces?
5. What did the Notes do when they realized that the gift of music was actually within them?

ACTIVITIES:

1. Play "I Am The Sweet Song." As they listen, write a few key words or lines on the board for discussion. (What do the words "I Am The Sweet Song" mean? What do the words "dancing Notes and a voice bring this song through" mean?)

VOCABULARY:

Ostinato
A phrase which is repeated consistently in succession.

I AM THE SWEET SONG

I am the sweet song I share with you.
I paint the melodies you can sing too.
Notes of all ages make your song come through.
Flitter free, like a bird, ahhh.

I am the sweet song I share with you.
I sing the melodies you can sing too.
Dancing Notes and a voice bring this song through.
Like a bird, soar with me, ahhh.

I am the sweet song I share with you.
Notes dance on lines and in spaces for you.
Musical journey takes flight in your mind.
Like a bird, soar with me, ahhh.

EXCERPT P (pages 34 and 35)
A Name For The Lines And Spaces

34

They understood that the **Pitches**
from each line and space
would now have to be sung
when danced upon.

So, while some **Notes** danced,
others would watch, and share in song.
Soon, the Music Castle would be filled
with sweet serenade.

The children decided it was time
to name the lines and spaces
that were within the castle.
They felt this creation should be named
after the Land Of Staff,
because of the colourful hills, mountains
and valleys in their surroundings
which inspired their music.

Yes, from then on,
it was to be called the **Staff.**

35

EXCERPT P (pages 34 and 35)
A Name For The Lines And Spaces

STORYLINE:

They realized that some Notes would have to dance on the lines and spaces as others would sing. The children decided that it was time to name the creation which the Music Fairy had given them. Because their land, with its hills and valleys, inspired their music, they decided to call the lines and spaces the "Staff." They gathered together to celebrate the new name in song.

MUSIC:

The feeling of the previous song is maintained with a simple melody and a small **ensemble** of instruments. As the key characters are mentioned, subtle reprises of the music used in the introductions of these characters are heard. Now, near the end of the story, these characters, each unique, have come together to enable the Notes to share their gift of music.

ILLUSTRATION:

The illustration on page 34 of the story book shows some of the scenery which inspired the naming of the Staff.

OBJECTIVES:

*   To introduce the name "Staff" for the lines and spaces.
*   To show that musical inspiration can come from many sources (in this case, from the mountains, hills and valleys of their land).
*   To show the importance of Clefs, Staff and rules, in making music.

FOR DISCUSSION:

1. What did they decide to call the lines and the spaces?
2. While some Notes danced on the Staff, what were the others to do?
3. What inspired their music in the Land Of Staff?
    (mountains, hills, valleys, etc.)
4. Draw a hill on the board. "Imagine that the hill is a melody. What happens to the melody as I go up the hill? Down the hill?" Do the same exercise with a valley.

ACTIVITIES:

1. Using the previously drawn Staff, or a new one, have the children draw some scenery directly on the lines and spaces. Looking at several of their drawings, discuss how the melodies would move (up or down) on their hills and valleys. Demonstrate these with your voice or on a piano, or perhaps one of the children would like to try. It is not important to have a beautiful melody. We only wish to track the general rise and fall of pitch.

VOCABULARY:

Ensemble
A small group of musicians, either instrumentalists or singers.

EXCERPT Q (pages 36 and 37)

The Dancing Note Song

Everyone was pleased,
and prepared to celebrate the new name
for the Music Fairy's gift.

Mr. and Mrs. Clef gathered the **Notes** together.

Mrs. Treble Clef then said . . .
"I would like some of the **Eighth Notes**,
Quarter Notes, and **Half Notes** up here with me."

Mr. Bass Clef got some of the **Whole Notes**
in his bottom section of the **Staff**.

They all began to dance and sing.

EXCERPT Q (pages 36 and 37)
The Dancing Note Song

STORYLINE:

The Notes sing a four-part song which can be performed as a **round**. The Eighth Notes begin, joined by the Quarter Notes, then the Half Notes, and finally, the Whole Notes. Each Note group has its own four measure melody.

MUSIC:

A very stylized harpsichord introduction sets the mood for the song which follows. Although each Note group has a different melody and different words, when repeated together, they all work to produce sounds which are very pleasant to the ear. Each Note group melody is comprised entirely of Notes from that specific Note group. Thus the listener can hear the differences in duration of each type of Note.

ILLUSTRATION:

The illustration is the music for the song, correctly notated on the Staff. The relationship of one Note type to the next is visually obvious here. One Whole Note = Two Half Notes = Four Quarter Notes = Eight Eighth Notes.

OBJECTIVES:

• To relate sound to the symbols of written music, showing the importance of the Clefs, Notes, and Staff in creating and performing music.

• To show the relationships of the various Note types to each other.

• To teach the children to perform a simple round which will produce some beautiful chord sounds when all parts are sung together.

FOR DISCUSSION:

1. The song we just heard started with the youngest Notes in the Land Of Staff. Who were they? Which Notes sang next? last?

2. Play the song again and have the children listen to the Eighth Note part. How many times do they repeat their melody? Do the same with the other three parts, i.e., Quarter, Half and Whole.

ACTIVITIES:

1. Teach each section of four measures to everyone. The sections can be combined in two ways. You may divide the class into four groups, assigning a different section to each group, and perform the song as on the CD. Or, you may do it as a round, like "Frère Jacques," with each group in turn beginning with the Eighth Note section and continuing through each section to the end of the Whole Notes.

2. Have the children hop together, from one foot to the other, with each syllable of the words. They may do this with the CD, as a preliminary or separate activity, or while singing. Be sure they all start on the same foot.

VOCABULARY:

Round
A song made up of sections of equal length which are meant to be sung together. "Row, Row, Row, Your Boat" is another example.

EXCERPT R (pages 38 and 39)
"Come Float With Me" Reprise

38

The skies were once again of sunlit sparkles,
and smiles spread far across the island,
while the people listened to the music
ringing from the castle — the joyous sounds
that echoed from one heart to another.

From this day forward,
the island was filled with song,
and all things were at peace.

39

EXCERPT R (pages 38 and 39)
"Come Float With Me" Reprise

STORYLINE:

The island is once again filled with song that echoes from one heart to another, and all things are at peace.

MUSIC:

The childrens' voices singing "sweet song I share" in the background, provide a serene ambiance for the closing narration, and prepare the listener for the voyage back home to reality from the island. This leads into the "Come Float With Me" reprise. The instrumental introduction is now augmented with **percussion** sounds which give more vitality to the song. A larger choir, throughout the body of the song, gives the sense of a joyous ending to a fantastic musical journey, and the anticipation of the next visit to the Land Of Staff.

ILLUSTRATION:

The Music Castle has now been added to this illustration of the island. The breeze is floating away from the island, ready to carry the listener home. The stars are still dancing in the skies.

OBJECTIVES:

• To show the children that, with the use of imagination, they were able to journey to a magical, musical land, meet some unique musical characters, and then return home with a sense of hope and new musical understanding.

FOR DISCUSSION:

1. What made all the happiness possible at the end of the story?
   (hard work, cooperation, sharing, listening)

ACTIVITIES:

1. As in the "Come Float With Me" intro, have the children imagine that they are floating on the breeze away from the island this time as their journey comes to an end.

VOCABULARY:

Percussion Instruments
Instruments which are sounded by striking or shaking.

COME FLOAT WITH ME (Reprise)

Come float with me on the warm soft breeze.
Return with me to a time long ago.
Let's drift across the sapphire sea
to reach an island waiting for you and me.

Chorus:
Magical, musical journey takes flight.
In your mind are no limits
to where we will climb.

Come soar with me through the winds of time.
Sail swiftly now, little wings of song.
Stay safe upon an angel's flight.
Fly with the echoes of sweet music's refrain . . .

Bridge:
Ah...

Come float with me on the warm soft breeze.
Come dance with me on the sunlit rays.
Embrace your dreams with reality.
Hold fast to the memory now and forever more . . .

Place the correct sticker in the circle provided for each of the following:

1. One of the Eighth Notes in the Land Of Staff looks like this...

2. One of the Quarter Notes in the Land Of Staff looks like this...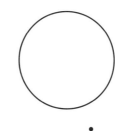

3. One of the Half Notes in the Land Of Staff looks like this...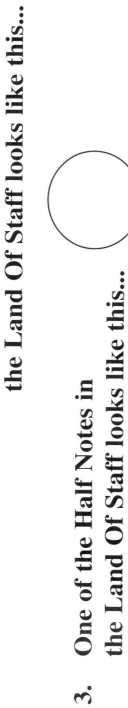

4. One of the Whole Notes in the Land Of Staff looks like this...

5. Mrs. Treble Clef looks like this...

6. Mr. Bass Clef looks like this...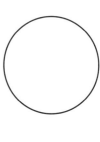

7. **The Music Fairy looks like this...**

8. **One of the half-year-old Notes looks like this...**

9. **Two of the half-year-old Notes, when joined together, look like this...**

10. **One of the one-year-old Notes looks like this...**

11. **One of the two-year-old Notes looks like this...**

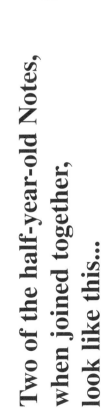

12. **One of the four-year-old Notes looks like this...**

THE STORY AS A WHOLE

ADDITIONAL ACTIVITIES:

1. Using the entire reproducible activity sheet, have the children draw the appropriate characters or, cut the sheet into sections, one for each student, and have the student choose the correct sticker (if available).

2. Create a different ending for the story after the Music Fairy takes the sounds away from the lines and spaces. This can be done in picture form.

3. Teach the students the "Dancing Note Song." In an advanced class, have the children create new lyrics for each musical line.

4. Create a class mural which includes the concepts learned from the story (working together, cooperation, sharing, listening, happiness). The drawings need not revolve around music-making.

5. If the children wish to share their responses with the author, have them compile their letters and mail them to:

> Paula Lynn Walker
> R.R. #2 Millbrook
> Millbrook, Ontario
> L0A 1G0

REFERENCES

Adler, Samuel. *The Study of Orchestration*. 2nd ed.
New York, London: W. W. Norton and Company, 1989.

Apel, Willi. *Harvard Dictionary of Music*. 2nd ed.
Cambridge, Massachusetts: The Belknap Press of Harvard University Press, 1969.

Feldstein, Sandy. *Pocket Dictionary of Music Terms Composers Theory*. 2nd ed.
Alfred Publishing Co., Inc., U.S.A.

Grout, Donald Jay. *A History of Western Music*, 3rd ed. with Claude V. Paliska.
New York, London: W. W. Norton and Company, 1980.

Blom, Eric, ed. *Grove's Dictionary of Music and Musicians*, 5th ed.
New York, London: St. Martin's Press, MacMillan & Co. Ltd., 1954.

CREDITS

Editing by Susan Tanner – my special thanks to her.
Thank you also to Joan Cobbold for her creative input in this Guide.